S0-DPF-671

Dedicated to
all children
around the
world

Japan
Spain
Ghana
India
Saudi Arabia
Russia
China
Mexico
Holland
Thailand
Scotland
USA

www.mascotbooks.com

Mr. Toad's Adventures: My First Doctor Visit

©2020 Tim Carpenter. All Rights Reserved. No part of this publication may
be reproduced, stored in a retrieval system or transmitted in any form by
any means electronic, mechanical, or photocopying, recording or otherwise
without the permission of the author.

For more information, please contact:
Mascot Books
620 Herndon Parkway, Suite 320
Herndon, VA 20170
info@mascotbooks.com

Library of Congress Control Number: 2020904672

CPSIA Code: PRTWP0720A
ISBN-13: 978-1-64543-407-8

Printed in South Korea

MR. TOAD'S ADVENTURES

MY First Doctor Visit

Tim Carpenter

Illustrated by Rachel Novel

"Professor Toad, what should I expect during my first doctor visit tomorrow?" asked Little Tadpole.

With a bright smile and a wave of his hand, Professor Toad asked Little Toran Toad to have a seat.

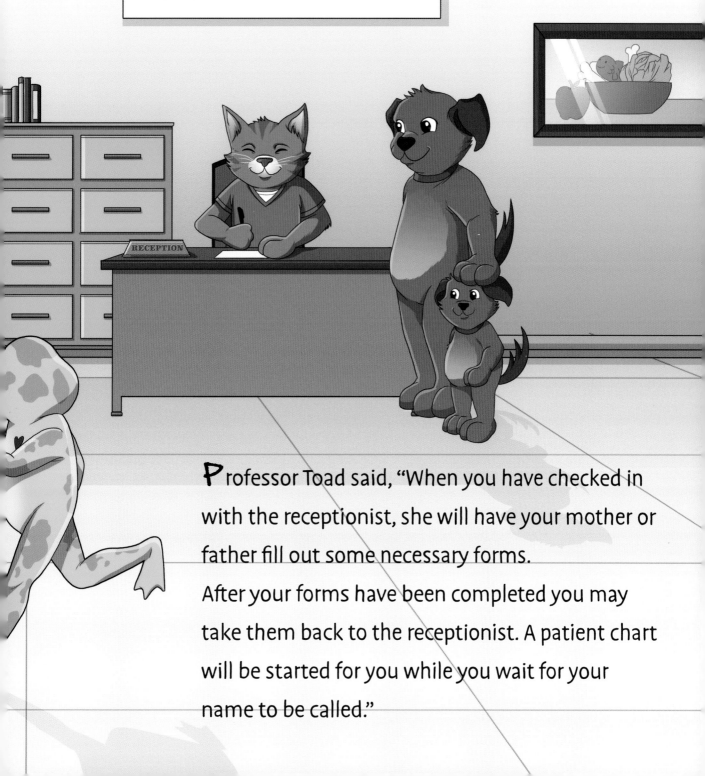

RECEPTION

Professor Toad said, "When you have checked in with the receptionist, she will have your mother or father fill out some necessary forms.

After your forms have been completed you may take them back to the receptionist. A patient chart will be started for you while you wait for your name to be called."

"When your name is called, a nurse will take you to an examination room and record your height, weight, temperature, blood pressure, heart rate, and respirations. Then, the nurse will ask you about the reason for your visit," Professor Toad says with a kind smile.

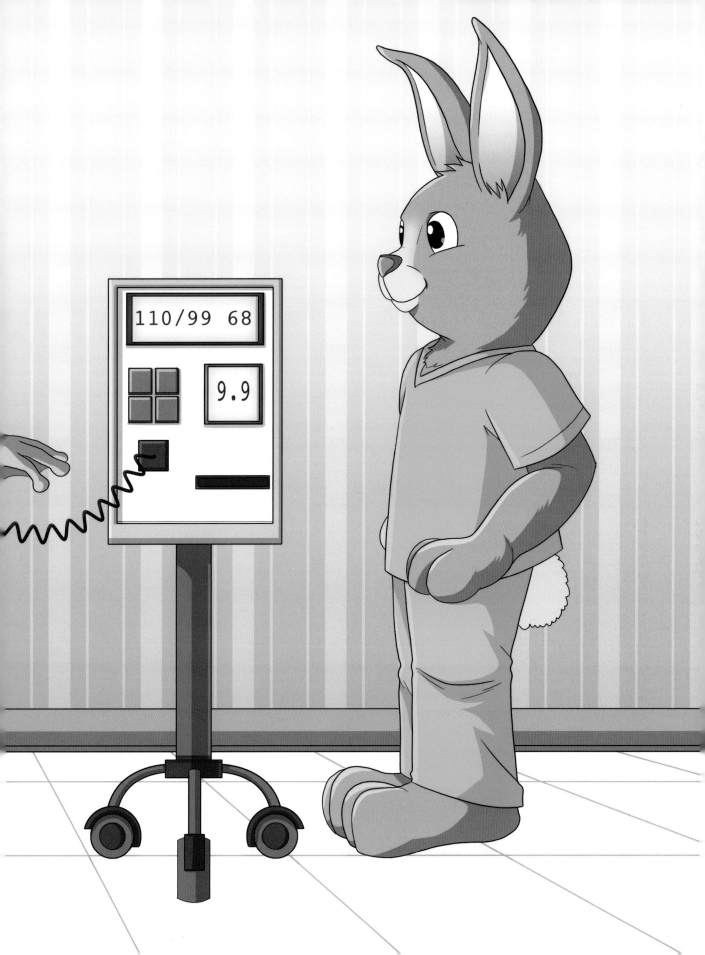

"Next, the nurse will have you go to another room to wait for the doctor.

When the doctor arrives, you will be asked more questions."

"The doctor will examine your ears, eyes, nose, and mouth, and listen to your heart, lungs, and stomach sounds," Professor Toad continued.

"The doctor will then examine you for muscle control by moving your arms and legs around to see your range of motion without pain," explained Professor Toad.

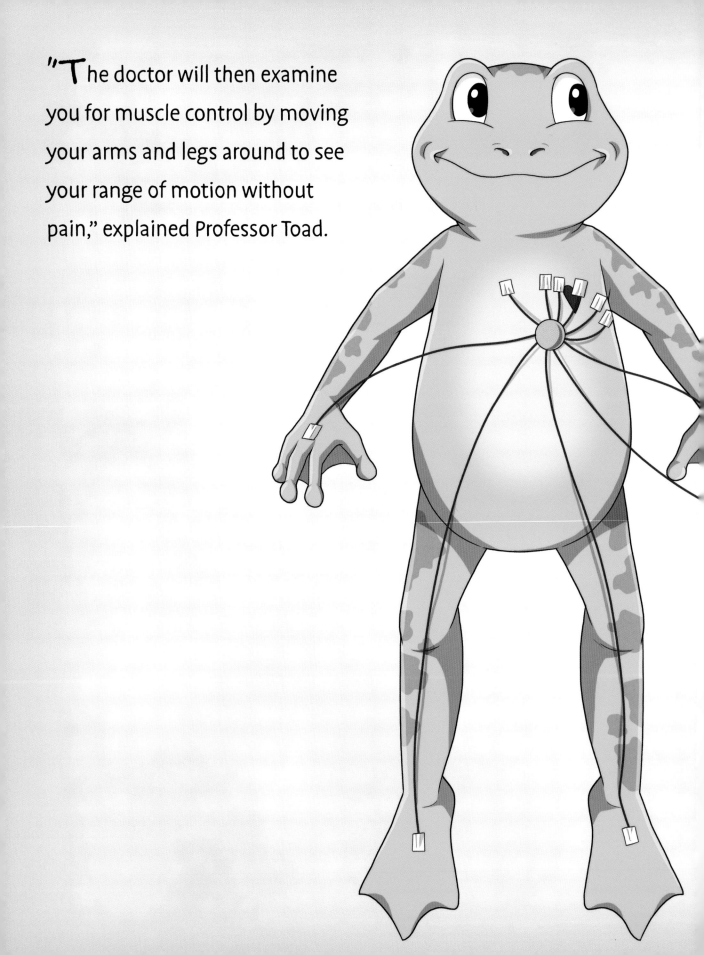

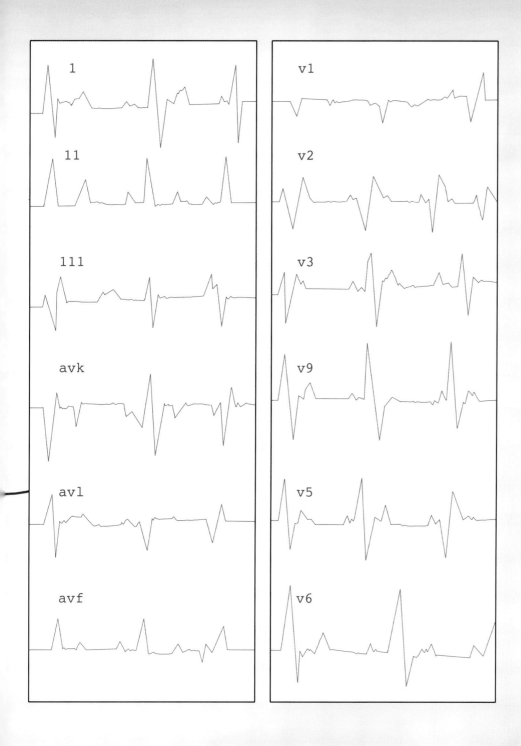

"After you're examined, a specialized test like an electrocardiogram (EKG) may be ordered. This test is to check the electrical activity of your heart."

"An x-ray may also be ordered. This allows the doctors to see your bones, lungs, blood vessels, and other organs," explained Professor Toad.

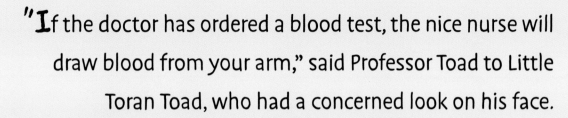

"If the doctor has ordered a blood test, the nice nurse will draw blood from your arm," said Professor Toad to Little Toran Toad, who had a concerned look on his face.

Professor Toad reassured Little Toran Toad, saying, "Specialized test results will be reviewed with you and your parents by the doctor. If necessary, your doctor may refer you to a specialist like an eye doctor or dentist."

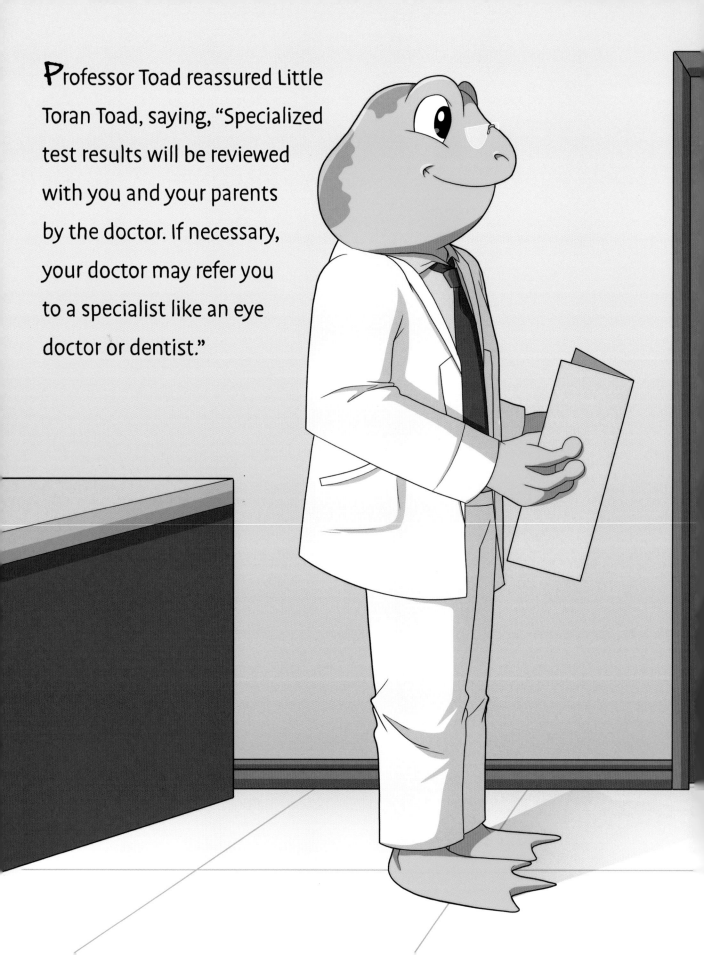

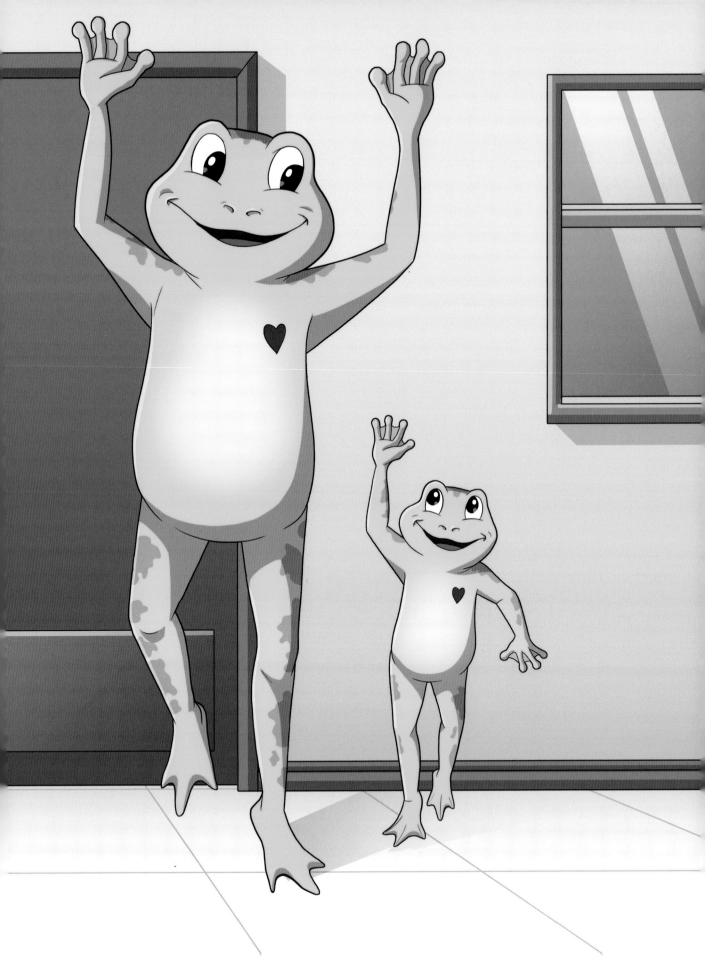

My First Doctor Visit

Date:

Doctor Practice:

Doctor Name:

Height:

Weight:

Blood Pressure:

Heart Rate:

Respiration:

Temperature:

Comments from your Doctor:

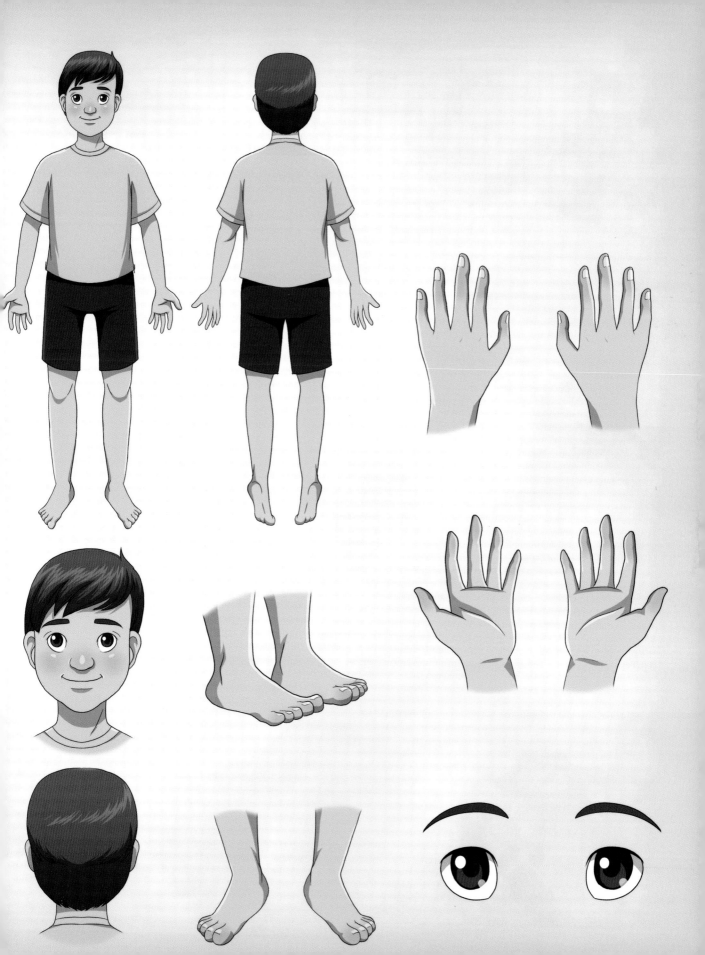

About the Author

Timothy Carpenter served in the U.S. Navy for twenty-four years. He retired as an Operation Specialist Chief Petty Officer, SW/AW. He received multiple awards while serving his country, including one Navy Commendation medal, five Navy Achievement medals, and many others. Once retired, he dedicated his life to saving lives in the medical field as an Emergency Medical Technician--Intermediate. He has experienced much and decided he wanted to share some of his positive experiences through his storybooks. Tim enjoys using his creative mind to create stories to enlighten young minds and encourage questions that build confidence in the young. Timothy Carpenter resides in Fredericksburg, Virginia with his two daughters and six grandchildren.